Reycraft Books
55 Fifth Avenue
New York, NY 10003

Reycraftbooks.com

Reycraft Books is a trade imprint and trademark of Newmark Learning, LLC.

This edition is published by arrangement with China Children's Press &
Publication Group Co., Ltd, China.
© China Children's Press & Publication Group Co., Ltd

English translation in the United States © 2021 Reycraft Books

Educators and Librarians: Our books may be purchased in bulk
for promotional, educational, or business use. Please contact
sales@reycraftbooks.com.

This is a work of fiction. Names, characters, places, dialogue, and incidents
described either are the product of the author's imagination or are used
fictitiously. Any resemblance to actual persons, living or dead, is entirely
coincidental.

Library of Congress Control Number: 2021902284

ISBN: 978-1-4788-7411-9

Printed in Dongguan, China. 8557/0421/17800

10 9 8 7 6 5 4 3 2 1

First Edition Hardcover published by Reycraft Books 2021

Reycraft Books and Newmark Learning, LLC, support diversity and
the First Amendment, and celebrate the right to read.

A Summer Night Concert

XIREN TONG

ILLUSTRATED BY SIXIN CHENG

Hands of Spring

Spring has a pair of tender hands.

It breaks the eggshells with gentle knocks.

It caresses the wet wings of baby birds and the

dandelion-like fluff of chicks and ducklings.

It opens the beehive. Those bees, awakened

from the winter period, fly out and

shake their transparent wings in

the golden sunshine.

Spring has a pair of wet hands. It plays tricks on the snow water dropping from the eaves, on the mountain frog that croaks like a naughty child, on the pitter-pattering rainfall that whispers softly, and on the mirrorlike lake that ripples on its surface.

Spring has a pair of warm hands.

It quietly removes the frozen soil

to let grass and flowers sprout from

the ground. It combs winter

wheat's tangled hair and braids

the tall plants near the water's edge.

It speeds the blooming of the buds,

which are like children's whistling

mouths, in the branches of peach,

plum, apricot, and pear trees.

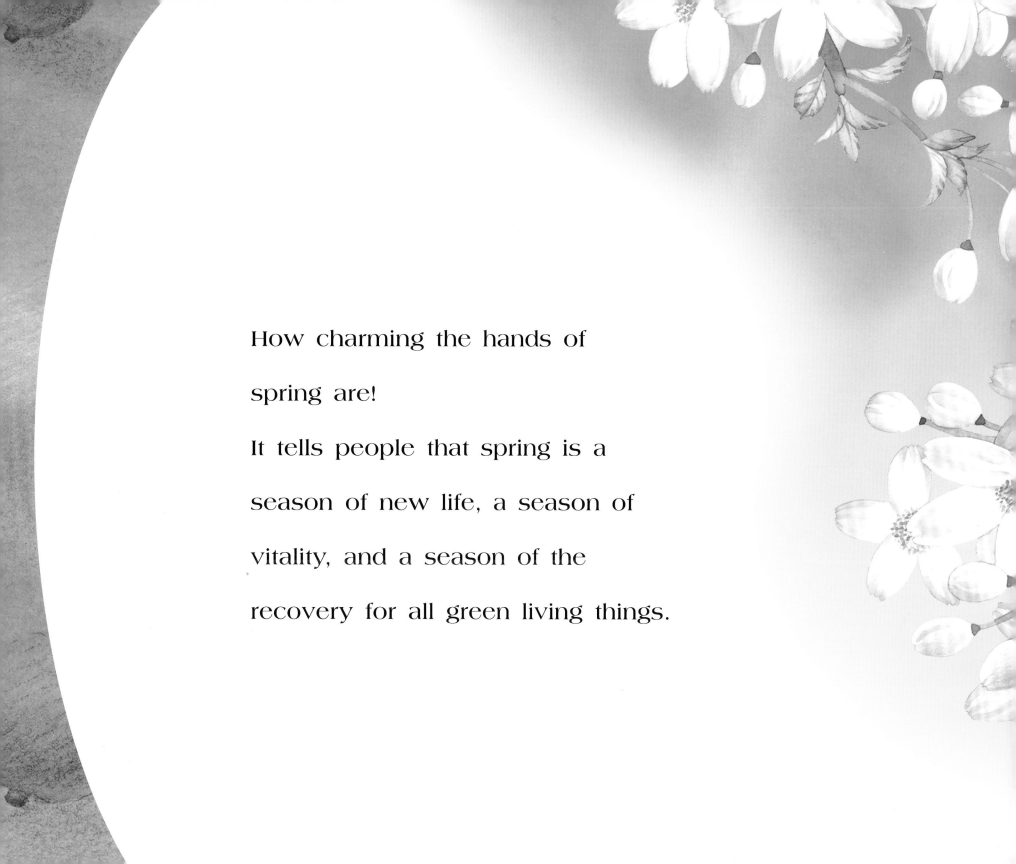

How charming the hands of
spring are!

It tells people that spring is a
season of new life, a season of
vitality, and a season of the
recovery for all green living things.

Carrying Cotton Baskets
on Our Heads

When our mother passed on, she gave each of us a little snow-white velvet umbrella.

"Dear children, go and fly," she said. "With Granny Wind's help, fly as far as you can. Remember, as long as there is soil, it is our home."

With Mother's last words, we began to fly.
We flew over rivers. We flew over mountains.
We flew until it was time to land.

The next year, as the sun caressed us and the spring rains fed us, we began to sprout. Soon, we wore the same green dress and the same golden flower crown as our mother once did.

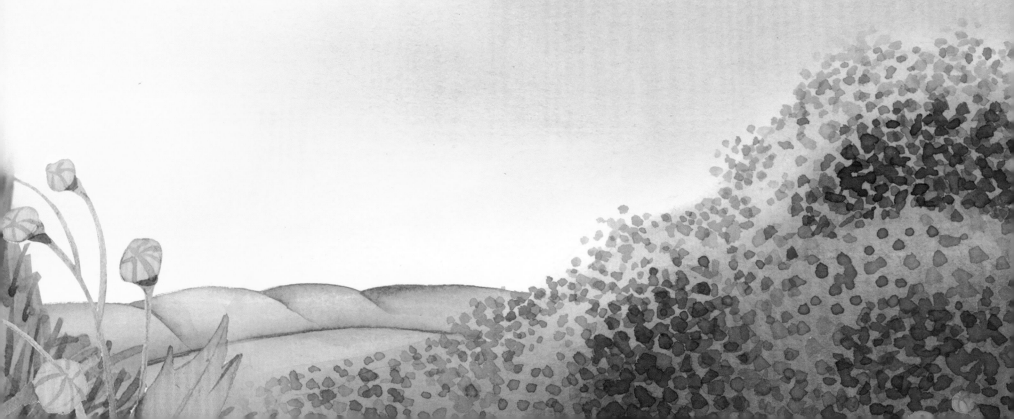

When autumn came, we stood on the hills and by the roadsides, holding our snow-white cotton baskets, looking into the distance as our mother once did.

It was then we heard children running and yelling. "Look at those beautiful dandelions!" They blew and blew, sending us into the waiting sky. Then we said goodbye to our own children, sending them everywhere as our mother once did to us.

A
Summer
Night
Concert

It is nearly silent in the field during a summer night. Auntie Moon pours her silver light into the pond and over the rice field. The water sparkles. Granny Wind carries the fragrance of flowers and a message that the summer night concert has started.

How beautiful the concert is...
until someone comes to poach for frogs.
Grandpa Owl shouts: "Don't catch our
field guards!"

The poacher flees in fear. The concert
starts again. How beautiful and joyful
the field is on a fragrant summer night.

Autumn Is a Ripe Pomegranate

Autumn is a ripe pomegranate that smiles all the time. It smiles because Mother Corn embraces her children even though they have already grown whiskers. It smiles because the beans tucked in their pods chatter in the winds as if they cannot wait to break free.

Autumn is a ripe pomegranate that smiles all the time. It smiles because the charming pumpkins and newly dug sweet potatoes lie happily naked. It smiles because the peppers glow red and green in the daytime as if they are looking for something.

Autumn is a ripe pomegranate
that smiles all the time. It smiles
because the waist-bending Mother
Trees in the orchard are proud—not
sad—as they watch trucks carrying
away their fruits. Their children.

Sunshine

Oh sunshine resting on the clouds, tell me what color you are.

When you shine on the lotus leaves, the silver dewdrops become sparkling and bright.

When you shine on the orchard, the apples blush their faces.

When you shine on the vegetable garden, you paint the pumpkins yellow, the eggplants purple, and the kidney bean flowers red.

Oh sunshine resting on the clouds, you are silly like a grandpa playing a magic trick. I wonder what this magic-trick playing grandpa will be like in the evening.

One day, some sunshine was hidden in a little box near the beach. The next morning, a curious kitten knocked the box of sunshine onto the floor. But where did the sunshine go?

The kitten stood at the window and mewed at the dawn light slowly appearing. Did the sunshine become this soft morning light?

Colorful Rain

Colorful rain in the summer falls slowly from the sky.

Like a naughty child, it quietly hides in the clouds, holding a shower nozzle in its hands and spraying water on the ground.

Pitter-patter.

The farm crops take a cold shower. Sprouts burst forth lush and sturdy overnight as if they have been fully fed.

Pitter-patter.

The fruits in the orchard are
now clean and beautiful. They sit
gorgeously dressed like little children.

Pitter-patter.

In the vegetable garden, red
tomatoes, purple eggplants,
green watermelons, and orange
pumpkins wear brighter colors
than ever before.

Pitter-patter.

Raindrops bounce and jump on children's umbrellas, creating colorful and magical pictures.

Each year, the rain of summer carries hope and joy, falling slowly from the sky.

The Wind Softly Says

The wind softly says into the girl's ear, "Raspberries are ripe in the mountain." The happy girl flits like a butterfly. She runs up the mountain with her friends, carrying a bamboo basket.

Colorful dresses flicker among the green plants. Joyous laughter shakes the dew off the grasses. The girls pick and pick. The thorns sting their fingers and the dewdrops splash their clothes as they fill the basket with ruby raspberries. And on the way home, the only sound is their chatter and laughter.

The wind softly says into the boy's ear, "Plums are ripe in the mountains." The boy runs up the mountain with his friends, climbing up trees like a bunch of monkeys. They pick plums and tuck these golden-red pearls into their pockets, bags, and watering mouths. On the way home, they chatter about the delicious plum cakes their mothers will bake. Oh, the fantastic days of summer!